TEENAGE MUTANT NINJA TURTLES

FOUR'S A CROWD

by J-P Chanda
illustrated by Let's Draw Studio

Simon Spotlight
New York   London   Toronto   Sydney

Based on the TV series *Teenage Mutant Ninja Turtles*™ as seen on Fox and Cartoon Network®

SIMON SPOTLIGHT
An imprint of Simon & Schuster Children's Publishing Division
1230 Avenue of the Americas, New York, New York 10020

One night at the Turtles' lair Master Splinter was leading the Teenage Mutant Ninja Turtles in a teamwork exercise. At least he was *trying* to lead.

"Hey!" shouted Leonardo. "You're supposed to work *with* me, Raphael!"

"But my way is better!" Raphael shouted back.

"Guys! Chill out!" yelled Michelangelo, trying to calm them down.

"Raph, you don't know the first thing about teamwork!" exclaimed Leonardo, angrily.

"Maybe I don't need a team!" replied Raphael.

"Well, maybe we don't need you, either!" Leonardo shouted.

"Good! I quit!" Raphael exclaimed and stormed out. The others tried to stop him, but Master Splinter held them back.

"He must choose his own path," Splinter explained, "wherever it takes him."

Raphael headed to the rooftops. He leaped from building to building with only the moonlight to guide him. He was alone. No one could boss him around anymore.

Who needs those guys anyway?, he thought to himself.

Back at the lair the next problem popped up on the monitors.

"Um, guys, check this out," Donatello said, pointing to the screens. There were Hun and some Foot Ninjas breaking into the museum.

The three crept into the museum and watched from the shadows. Hun and his soldiers were breaking into an enormous vault.

"That's where the city's most precious diamond is stored," Donatello whispered.

"They must be trying to swipe it," Michelangelo said.

"Let's get 'em!" hissed Leonardo.

As soon as the vault was open, the Turtles leaped into action.

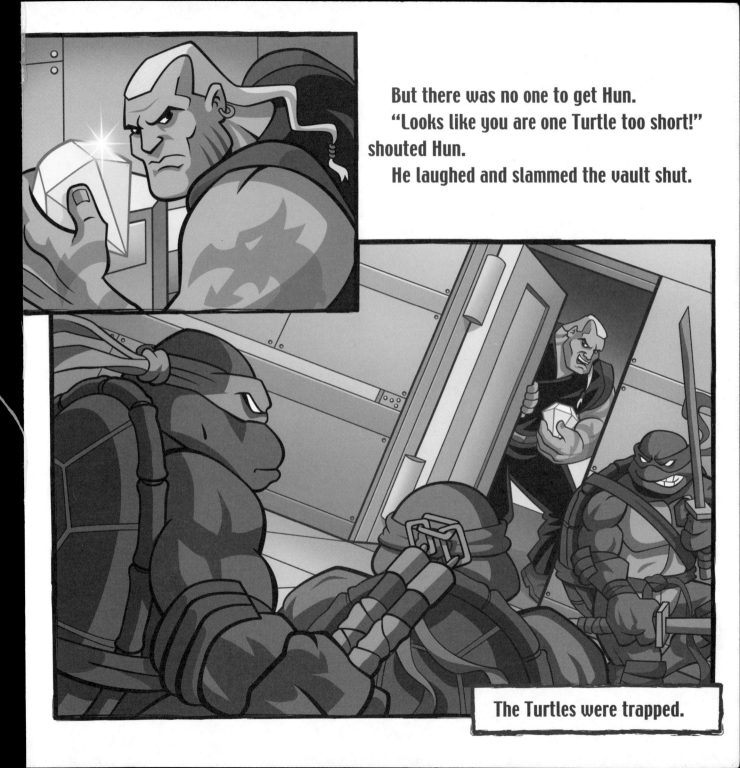

But there was no one to get Hun.

"Looks like you are one Turtle too short!" shouted Hun.

He laughed and slammed the vault shut.

The Turtles were trapped.

Master Splinter saw everything on the monitors. He reached for his Shell Cell phone and said, "Raphael, your brothers need you . . . the museum . . . hurry!"

But Splinter was not sure if he heard the message. Raphael did not answer.

The air in the vault was quickly running out.
"I guess this is it," Donatello gasped.
"Save your breath," said Leonardo.
"For what?" asked Michelangelo.

"For some serious shelling!" Raphael answered, as he threw open the vault's door. Air rushed into the room. The Turtles got to their feet.

"If it wasn't for you, we'd be goners!" Leonardo cried.

"But we all need to work together to stop Hun," said Raphael.

"Making up is totally sweet," Michelangelo interrupted. "But putting the smackdown on the bad guys would be even sweeter!"

Hun and his gang were busy stealing as many artifacts as they could carry. But outside the museum Donatello, Leonardo, and Michelangelo were waiting for them to try to escape.

"You three aren't enough to stop me!" Hun gloated.

"Good thing there are *four* of us!" cried Raphael, as he swooped down and snatched the diamond.

With all four Turtles working together the Foot Ninjas didn't stand a chance.

Hun managed to creep away, but without any of the artifacts he was after . . . or any of his soldiers.

Later that night Splinter welcomed Raphael back to the lair. "The path of success lies with your family," Splinter said softly.

"I know that now," answered Raphael.

"Me too," said Leonardo.

"Awesome!" said Michelangelo. "So who in this family is making me dinner?"

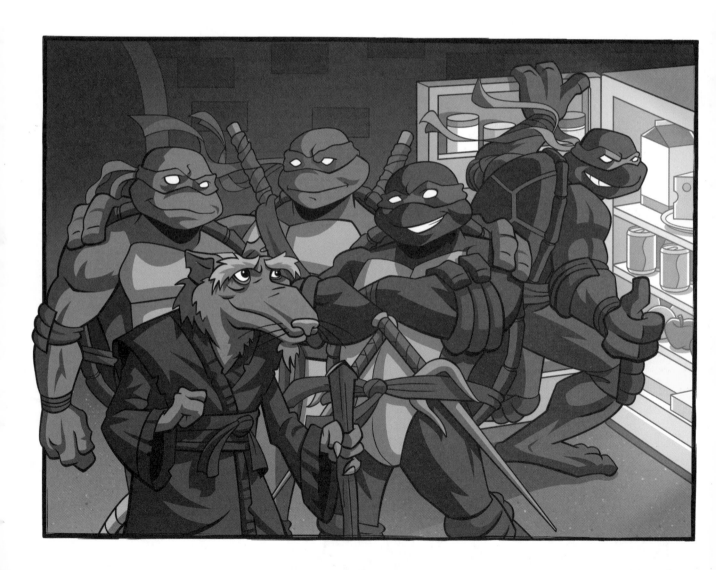